A book is a treasure we keep in our memory chest...
This treasure belongs to:

_____

To My Beloved, Who Was The Light of Day

Published by Faux Paw Media Group, A Division of Faux Paw Productions, Inc.™

www.fauxpawproductions.com

Composed in the United States of America
Printed in China

First Impression 2006
ISBN 978-0-9777340-4-7
SAN: 850-637x

Library of Congress Cataloging-in-Publication Data

Carman, Debby
Kittywimpuss - Got Game / written and illustrated by Debby Carman

Summary: A cat with low self-esteem and no confidence learns that participation in play is as rewarding as winning.
(1. Cats-Fiction. 2. Stories in Rhyme. 3. Sportsmanship - fiction)
I. Title   II. Carman, Debby

Kittywimpuss, Got Game

A parable written and illustrated by Debby Carman©

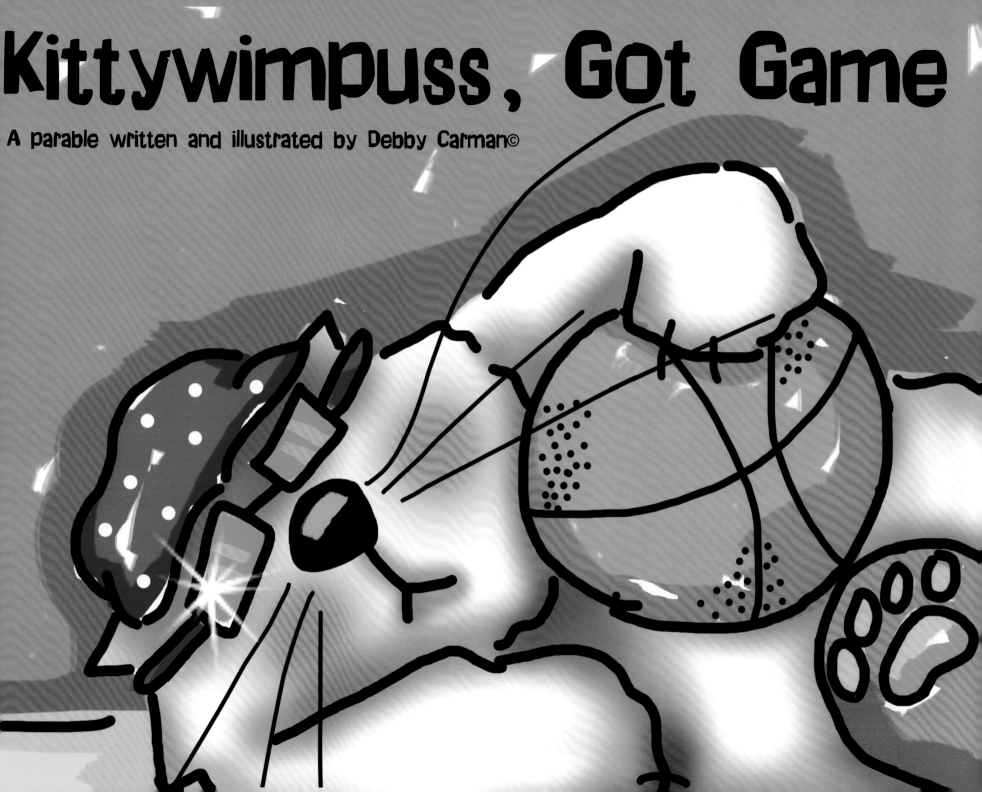

This is a story of one attitude cat
in a rumply fur suit and a red polka dot hat.

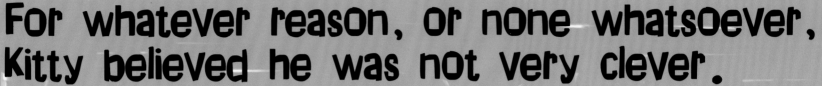

For whatever reason, or none whatsoever,
Kitty believed he was not very clever.

"Making a fuss, a definite must!"

Deep down in your heart,
your want to be part.
Under that wooly shag fur,
You're hiding a purr!

Smile ear to ear even if you're last in line.

Don't let your doubt
make you sit the game out.